For Bella Jean, Laurel and Carla –
inspirational big sisters! AMQ
For Christine and Charlie, RB

First published in paperback in the UK in 2011 by
Alanna Books
46 Chalvey Road East,
Slough, Berkshire, SL1 2LR

www.alannabooks.com

ISBN: 978-1-907825-04-0
Printed and bound in China

Lulu reads to Zeki

Anna McQuinn
Illustrated by Rosalind Beardshaw

ALANNA BOOKS

Lulu's day always ends with a story.

Tonight, her mummy reads one about
a little girl and her new baby brother.

Lulu's mummy is having a new baby, too.
Lulu is going to be a big sister.

Mummy's tummy gets bigger and bigger.

But she still has time to read with Lulu.
Lulu chooses stories the baby will like.

Daddy makes new shelves for the baby's things and Lulu sorts her books.
Some are for keeping...

...and some are for the new baby.
She puts them on the new shelf
with her duck and her old teddy.

Then one day, the new baby arrives.
His name is Zeki.

Lulu brings him a soft book for his cot.
It's a perfect present for a new brother!

Lulu's new baby
brother cries a lot!

Lulu wants to cheer him up
so she tells him a story.

But it turns out he is
just hungry.

So, while Mummy feeds Zeki, Lulu holds her best bear story.
She and Mummy read it together.

Sometimes Zeki cries when he needs a new nappy.

Lulu reads him her best potty book.

Sometimes he cries in the bath.

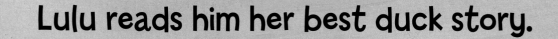

Lulu reads him her best duck story.

Sometimes Zeki cries when he's tired.
Lulu reads him her best sleepy story.

She sings a song for Zeki and then he goes to sleep.

Lulu's new baby brother sleeps a lot!

While he is sleeping Lulu plays
with her teddies.

Being a big sister is a big job.
Sometimes Lulu helps her mummy.

Sometimes she helps her daddy.
The new baby keeps everyone very busy.

But they are not too busy to
end the day with a story...

...for the best big sister of all.